Rory was throwing his basketball into the hoop on the side of his house when his friend Amelia ran out from the house next door, her eyes gleaming with excitement.

"You can stop that right now, Rory," she said. "The Pet Finders Agency has another case. Mrs Fraser from Lochside Boat Hire has just phoned. She and her family are about to go on holiday and they've lost Barney. They can't go on holiday without him."

"Barney," said Rory, catching the ball and trying to spin it round on his index finger. "Is that the big scruffy brown and white dog that's always eating? He's enormous."

Amelia nodded. "I've got an old lead, but we'd better go and collect his too. It might take two of us to haul him back if he's not keen. I'm going to change into my Pet Finders' gear. I'll see you at your front gate in ten minutes."

Amelia swiftly ran back indoors and dressed in her black jeans, black trainers and white T shirt with PFA stencilled on it. As usual she hung a torch, a mobile phone and a piece of rope onto her belt. These had come in useful on their first case when she and Rory had rescued a lost cat and some lemurs. She rolled up the old lead and stuffed it into her back pocket.

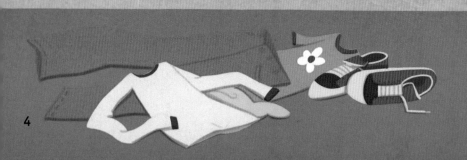

Rory was already dressed in his old jeans and a T shirt, but he went indoors and added a crash helmet, knee and elbow pads and some camouflage paint – an outfit he knew Amelia wouldn't approve of. His mum's old tartan cape completed the picture. He looked at himself in the hall mirror.

"Pet Finders to the rescue," he cried. "Yeah!"

Then he scowled as he glanced back out of the window. He was just a bit annoyed.

Amelia had put up a sign on her garden gate that said:

PET FINDERS AGENCY
OWNER
MISS AMELIA FUDGE

There was no sign of his name. While he admitted that the agency had initially been Amelia's idea, and that it had earned them some summer holiday pocket money and was exciting and good fun, he still felt it was unfair. He'd done half of the work and deserved to have his name on the sign too.

Rory went out of the house and met up with Amelia at his front gate.

Amelia looked at his outfit and was definitely not impressed.

"I don't see why you need to put paint on yourself," she said. "It's not as if we're going into the jungle."

"You never know what's out there," Rory shrugged. He liked his camouflage paint. It made him feel brave.

When they got down to the Lochside Boat Hire, Mrs Fraser was already waiting for them with Barney's lead.

"Our camper van's nearly packed and ready to go," she said, "but Barney's disappeared. One minute he was there; the next he was gone. We've searched all round the loch side but can't find him anywhere. The twins are very upset."

Amelia looked at the two tear-stained children clinging to their mother's skirt.

"Don't worry," she said to them, "we'll soon find Barney."

"That's right," agreed Rory. "The Pet Finders always get their man or dog or cat or lemurs. Did you hear the story about how we saved the lemurs ...?"

"Come on, Rory." Amelia pulled him away. "There's no time to chat now. Remember, this is business. Now let's get started."

They waved goodbye to the Fraser family and
set off.

"Where should we start looking?" asked Rory.

"Around all of the town's dustbins," said
Amelia.

"You think he might be stuck in one of them?"

"Don't be silly," said Amelia. "I think he might
have knocked them over looking for food."

"Yeuch!" said Rory. "I hate dustbins. They're
always really smelly." He sighed. "I should have
brought a clothes peg for my nose."

Chapter Two

The Pet Finders headed back along the loch side and into town to hunt for Barney.

"There are so many dustbins," groaned Rory. "Where on earth shall we start?"

"Shhhh ..." Amelia looked thoughtful for a moment and then began to look up at the sky.

"Barney can't fly," muttered Rory under his breath. "He's not likely to be up there."

"No," said Amelia sharply, "but the seagulls can fly. Look at them up there, wheeling round. I bet they've spotted food. Let's follow them."

They followed the seagulls, looking up every so often to check they were going in the right direction. Rory looked up once too often and ended up walking straight into a lamp post.

"Good thing I was wearing my crash helmet and knee pads," he grinned at Amelia.

Amelia sighed. "Come on, Rory. We haven't got all day."

The seagulls led them to the bakery where Amelia and Rory went down the little lane to the back of the shop. In the backyard, they found all the bins toppled over. The ground was strewn with empty bags of flour and sugar, and there were several margarine tubs which had been licked clean.

"Barney's definitely been here," concluded Amelia. "Look at those big floury paw prints. We're on the right trail. Let's try the gardens further up this street."

Amelia was right. At each house they went to, they found that all the bins had been pushed over and their contents scattered. The seagulls strutted around pecking at bits of rubbish and screeching their annoyance at the lack of food. A man came out to chase the seagulls and discovered Amelia and Rory inspecting the bin,

"Did you two make this mess?" he asked angrily.

"Certainly not," said Amelia indignantly, drawing herself up to her full height. "We are from the Pet Finders Agency and we are investigating the disappearance of a dog."

"Have you seen a large mongrel sniffing around?" Rory interrupted. "Big greedy hairy mutt with floppy ears?"

"Come to think of it, I did see a dog earlier," said the man, "and if I get hold of him ... just look at all this rubbish. It'll take me ages to put it back in the bin!"

"Sorry we can't stay to help you," said Amelia quickly, "but we really must be going. Come on, Rory. Barney can't be far away now."

The Pet Finders speeded up their search, passing pile after pile of strewn rubbish and upturned bins, but Barney always seemed to be one paw ahead of them. At last they came to a dustbin which was still standing upright.

"We must have passed him," said Rory. "He hasn't got to this one yet."

Amelia inspected the bin. "No, but something else has," she said. "Look!"

Chapter Three

Rory looked at the dustbin where a small yellow and black snake was curled up on top of the lid, sunning itself.

"Whoa!" said Rory, backing away quickly. "No wonder Barney didn't go near that dustbin. There's no way I'm going near it either. Come on, let's get out of here."

"Wait a minute," said Amelia. "That's not a native snake; it must be someone's pet."

"Pretty weird pet if you ask me ..." said Rory, still backing away.

Amelia continued, ignoring him. "It's a young ball python by the look of it. I recognise the markings from my animal kingdom book. They come from Africa but they're not poisonous. We could find its owner and return it. Who knows, there might be a reward and we are the Pet Finders, after all."

Rory looked doubtful. "But how are we going to return it?" he asked. "You can't put a snake on a lead."

"Of course not," scoffed Amelia. "They're great escape artists. They're all muscle and can squeeze through the tiniest of spaces so you have to catch them in some kind of bag. I read that in a book too."

Rory looked at Amelia's belt, but there was no bag hanging there.

That didn't stop Amelia. "I see a pillowcase on next door's washing line."

Before Rory could stop her, Amelia had gone over the fence, removed the pillowcase and brought it back.

A loud voice came over the fence, "What are you doing with that pillowcase?"

The angry owner of the pillowcase came charging out of her back door and demanded an answer. "Put it back this minute!"

"I'm sorry," said Amelia, in her best bossy voice, "but I'm afraid that's just not going to be possible. I'm from the Pet Finders Agency, you see, and there is a snake on the loose and I must borrow this pillowcase in order to catch it safely."

The woman looked puzzled.

"Of course I shall return it washed and ironed," added Amelia.

"You mean your mum will," muttered Rory.

The woman glanced over the fence and spotted the snake. "Oh dear!" she exclaimed, backing away. "All right ... but mind you bring it back. That pirate one is my grandson's favourite!"

Rory found two bamboo canes and carefully lifted the sleepy snake into the pillowcase. Amelia tied the top of the pillowcase securely in a knot.

"You can carry it," she said, thrusting the pillowcase at Rory.

Rory looked thoughtful. "No."

Amelia frowned at him, "Why not? Are you scared? I'm carrying the rope and the torch and the phone. It's only fair ..."

"I'll only carry it on one condition."

"Which is?"

"That you add my name to the sign on your gate. I'm half of the Pet Finders Agency." Then he added, "... It's only fair."

"Hmm, I'll think about it," said Amelia, surprised by Rory's sudden outburst. She really didn't fancy carrying the snake herself.

She was handing the snake over to Rory when a doggy face with big floppy ears suddenly appeared round the corner of the building. It was Barney.

"Come here this minute," ordered Amelia.

No chance. Barney picked up his big paws and took off like a rocket.

Amelia and Rory gave chase.

"Stop!" yelled Rory.

But he didn't. Barney loved chasing games and this was starting to look like it might be a good one.

Chapter Four

Amelia and Rory chased Barney all the way to the edge of the town. They dodged young women with prams, grannies with toddlers and teenagers with headphones as they ran along the pavements. They nearly lost Barney when they saw him knock over a tray of onions outside the greengrocers'. They insisted it wasn't their fault, but the greengrocer made them stop to pick up the onions anyway.

They nearly lost Barney again when he
shot across the road without waiting for the
safe signal.

"Doesn't that dog know anything!"
exclaimed Amelia, furiously.

Meanwhile, Rory was worried about the snake;
it was having quite a bumpy ride in its pirate
pillowcase. Did snakes get sick like humans? Did
they throw up? If so, what? Whole mice and
voles perhaps? He wasn't sure. He'd have to
ask Amelia. She would know. She always knew
everything ...

Finally, after running for ages, Barney came to a skidding halt by some community gardens. They were badly overgrown with grass and tall weeds and were obviously no longer used.

In the middle of the gardens was an ancient shed with peeling green paint. An old folding chair and a watering can sat quietly rusting outside the shed door while a faded sign said the shed was HAMISH'S HIDEOUT. The shed windows were grimy with dust and age, and one small pane at the very top had smashed and lay broken on the grass.

Out of breath after the long chase, Amelia made her way through the tall weeds and was the first to reach Barney. He was now standing with his front paws leaning against the garden shed, barking furiously. She took out both leads and clipped them on to his collar.

"Got you at last, you great mutt," she puffed. "This pet-finding is hard work."

Rory panted up beside her. Knee pads weren't great for running long distances in. He took hold of one of the leads.

"Come on, Barney," he said, "time to go home. Your family is worried about you and they want to take you on holiday." But Barney kept barking at the shed and wouldn't budge.

"Come along, Barney," said Amelia, in her sternest voice. "You need to walk back now. You're far too heavy for Rory to carry."

"Too right," muttered Rory. "I've already got a snake!" But Barney just kept staring at the shed and refused to move.

"Maybe he's tired," said Rory. "I know I am."

"Or maybe he thinks there's something inside," said Amelia.

Rory and Amelia listened, but they couldn't hear anything.

"Oh come on, Barney," Amelia was growing impatient. "We must go now." But Barney gave a warning growl from deep in his throat.

An answering warning growl came from inside the shed, enough to make Barney stop barking and back away.

GRRRRRR!

"It's another dog," cried Rory. "There must be another dog in there. That's what he can hear. Looks like we've got another dog to rescue. Good thing we brought two leads."

Amelia frowned. "There's only one thing that puzzles me," she said.

"What's that?" asked Rory.

"The door of the shed is closed and a chair is up against it. How did another dog get in?" Amelia asked quizzically.

"Maybe it's been locked in and abandoned," said Rory. "Horrible people do that sometimes."

"Well, there's only one way to find out," said Amelia. "Time for Pet Finders to investigate ..."

Chapter Five

"Investigate!" cried Rory excitedly. Then he hesitated. "But supposing there's a vicious dog in there and it attacks as soon as we open the door?"

"We have Barney to protect us," said Amelia.

Rory looked at Barney. He didn't look very brave and seemed an unlikely superhero.

"You're not scared, are you?" Amelia teased.

"Certainly not," said Rory. "I'm only thinking of the snake. We've just rescued it. We don't want it to be eaten by a mad dog."

"Okay. Then we'll go round the shed and see if there are any other ways in or out. That way we won't be taken by surprise. Come on, Barney."

Barney came, but they could tell by his flattened ears that he wasn't keen.

Slowly and carefully they worked their way through the weeds towards the old shed. When they got close, Rory handed the snake to Amelia, dropped to his hands and knees and began to crawl forward.

"You stay here," he whispered to Amelia.

"What are you doing?" hissed Amelia.

"I can get really close without being seen. Just like the commandos do. I'm wearing my camouflage paint, remember."

"You're also wearing a bright blue crash helmet and a tartan cape," said Amelia pointedly.

"Oh yeah, right." Rory stood up and took back the snake. "I'd forgotten about that."

Amelia shook her head. "We'll check out the back of the shed first. The tall weeds will give us some cover."

They tiptoed all the way round. The tall grasses tickled their noses and Rory sneezed.

"Atishoo!"

Barney took fright, leaped into the air and knocked over Amelia.

"Ow! You stupid mutt!" She clapped her hand over her mouth to stifle the yell. They edged forwards and all the way around the shed, but it only had one door. There was no other way in or out. Carefully, Rory tried to open the door. It was locked.

"We could try looking in the window," he suggested.

"They're too dirty. We won't be able to see a thing."

"We might be able to see in through the broken pane."

"If we were seven feet tall," said Amelia. "It's too high up."

"I could stand on your shoulders and look in," said Rory.

"I could stand on *your* shoulders and look in," said Amelia.

"I've got the crash helmet and the elbow pads," Rory pointed out.

"Okay." Amelia gave in. She tied Barney's leads to the shed doorknob while Rory put the snake carefully on the ground.

Amelia made a basket with her hands. Rory tried to climb up.

"What have you been eating?" complained Amelia. "You weigh a ton. Hurry up. I can't hold you much longer."

Rory heaved himself up and grabbed hold of the edge of the window ledge. He almost got a look in when ...

"EEEEAA ... AA ... AA ...!" A high pitched laugh rang out from the shed.

Rory got a fright and toppled over.

"Just as well you're wearing your crash helmet and elbow pads," remarked Amelia.

"This is too weird. I want to go home," moaned Rory.

Barney looked as though he agreed.

Chapter Six

"We can't give up now," said Amelia. "Remember what you told Mrs Fraser. Pet Finders always get their man or dog or cat ..."

"Or whatever it is that's in there ... it doesn't sound human or animal," muttered Rory.

"For goodness' sake, Rory, ghosts don't live in sheds," said Amelia. "I read that in a book." But she crossed her fingers behind her back as she said it.

AAR!

"Okay. I'll try again," agreed Rory. He hoisted himself back up and he almost got his eye to the broken window when ...

"RAAAAR!" A roar like an angry lion startled him and he fell off the shed and into a thick patch of overgrown nettles.

"Right, that's it," he said. "I don't care what's in there. I'm going home."

"Look," said Amelia. "I have another idea. Why don't we thread the rope through the lock on the shed door and pull? Then we can stand well clear of whatever's in there."

"No way …" Rory rubbed his nettle stings.

"I'll put your name on the Pet Finders sign," said Amelia.

Rory looked thoughtful. He did want his name on the sign. "Okay. Just one more go then," he agreed.

They threaded the rope through the rusty old lock and backed away as far as they could.

"Now pull," said Amelia.

They pulled harder and harder, until the door suddenly flew open and a noise like a trumpeting elephant almost deafened them. But no elephant came charging out. No lion either. Certainly not a hyena. Not even a dog.

"What on earth … " Amelia and Rory looked at each other.

"We have to find out," said Amelia.

Rory nodded and they slowly made their way to the shed and peered around the open door.

Inside, an African grey parrot was hopping about on a dusty old shelf.

"Good morning, boys and girls," he cackled.

Welcome to the zoo!

Rory and Amelia burst out laughing.

"He must have escaped from the zoo," said Amelia. "I bet he can imitate all the animals."

"I expect he flew in through the broken window," said Rory. "We'd better try to catch him and take him back. How about I throw my cape over him and we can wrap him up in it?"

Once the parrot was safely captured, they headed back into town carrying one snake, one parrot and leading one large dog.

"We always end up with more animals than we bargained for," grinned Amelia.

Chapter Seven

On their way back into town, Amelia phoned
Mrs Fraser to tell her the good news about
Barney. She was just hanging her phone back
on her belt when she got a text from her mum:

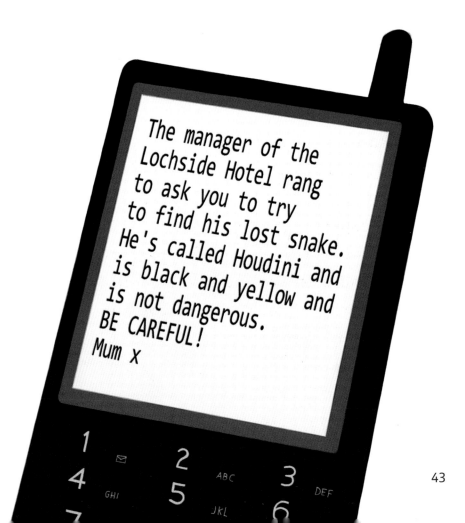

The manager of the
Lochside Hotel rang
to ask you to try
to find his lost snake.
He's called Houdini and
is black and yellow and
is not dangerous.
BE CAREFUL!
Mum x

Amelia showed the text to Rory. "We can take Houdini back at the same time as Barney. We pass the hotel on our way."

The manager of the hotel was delighted to get Houdini back. "I was just cleaning out his tank this morning," he said, "when he managed to slip away from me. I searched the grounds of the hotel but he had completely disappeared." He gave them a reward and two tickets to the special barbecue at the Lochside Hotel the following weekend.

"Thank you very much," smiled Amelia, pocketing the money.

"I love a good burger!" grinned Rory, pocketing the tickets.

RUFF! RUFF!

PFA

They carried on walking to the Lochside Boat Hire where Mrs Fraser and the twins were waiting.

"Oh Barney, you're back," cried the twins giving him a big hug.

Barney wagged his big bushy tail. "Ruff ruff," he answered.

"Ruff ruff," the tartan cape echoed back.

"What on earth ..." said an astonished Mrs Fraser.

Amelia explained all that had happened.

"We're going to take the parrot back to the zoo now," said Rory.

"I'll give you a lift if you like," said Mrs Fraser. "It's on my way."

Rory climbed into the car while Amelia phoned her mum to tell her what was happening.

When they arrived at the zoo, the zoo keeper was relieved to get her parrot back.

"He usually sits at the zoo entrance and welcomes everyone," she told Amelia, "but somehow he got loose. I'm delighted you found him. He's so tame that he couldn't have survived out there on his own. Here is a reward for finding him and two free tickets to the zoo."

Amelia and Rory were pleased with their day's work. Now they had plenty of pocket money for the summer holidays, a trip to the zoo and a barbecue to look forward to.

"Yes, it really was a good idea of mine to set up the Pet Finders Agency," said Amelia proudly when they got home.

"But you couldn't have rescued the animals without me," Rory pointed out.

"That's true," smiled Amelia. "I'll go and get the paint and the brush for the sign right now …"

Amelia wrote Rory's name under hers, then Rory took the paintbrush from Amelia and under their names he added ...

PET FINDERS AGENCY
OWNERS
MISS AMELIA FUDGE
and
MR RORY McTAVISH
(No animal too BIG or
too small or too SCARY!!!)